For Michal Sagar,
extraordinary artist and friend,
and for M., R., and C.

BEACH LANE BOOKS • An imprint of Simon & Schuster Children's Publishing Division • 1230 Avenue of the Americas, New York, New York 10020 • Copyright © 2016 by Lauren Stringer • Calligraphy by Judythe Sieck • All rights reserved, including the right of reproduction in whole or in part in any form. • BEACH LANE BOOKS is a trademark of Simon & Schuster, Inc. • For information about special discounts for bulk purchases, please contact Simon & Schuster Special Sales at 1-866-506-1949 or business@simonandschuster .com. • The Simon & Schuster Speakers Bureau can bring authors to your live event. For more information or to book an event, contact the Simon & Schuster Speakers Bureau at 1-866-248-3049 or visit our website at www.simonspeakers.com. • Book design by Lauren Rille • The text for this book was set in Banda. • The illustrations for this book were rendered in watercolor and acrylic paint on Arches oil paper. • Manufactured in China • 0716 SCP • First Edition • 10 9 8 7 6 5 4 3 2 1 • Library of Congress Cataloging-in-Publication Data • Names: Stringer, Lauren, author illustrator. • Title: Yellow time / Lauren Stringer. • Description: First edition. | New York : Beach Lane Books, [2016] | Summary: "A lyrical ode to that magical time in autumn when the leaves turn yellow"— Provided by publisher. • Identifiers: LCCN 2015029955| ISBN 9781481431569 (hardcover : alk. paper) | ISBN 9781481431576 (e-book) • Subjects: | CYAC: Autumn—Fiction. | Leaves—Fiction. • Classification: LCC PZ7.S9183 Ye 2016 | DDC [E]—dc23 LC record available at http://lccn.loc.gov/2015029955

Yellow Time

LAUREN STRINGER

Beach Lane Books • New York London Toronto Sydney New Delhi

The squirrels are too busy to notice.
And the geese have already gone.

Other birds have left too,
but not the crows.

Crows love yellow time.

They fill still-leafy trees
with their voices announcing
its coming to everyone.

Just before yellow time,
the air smells different.
Like wet mud and dry grass
with a sprinkle of sugar.

Yellow time comes
before white time.

Every time.

Everyone is ready.
The trees can't hold on forever.

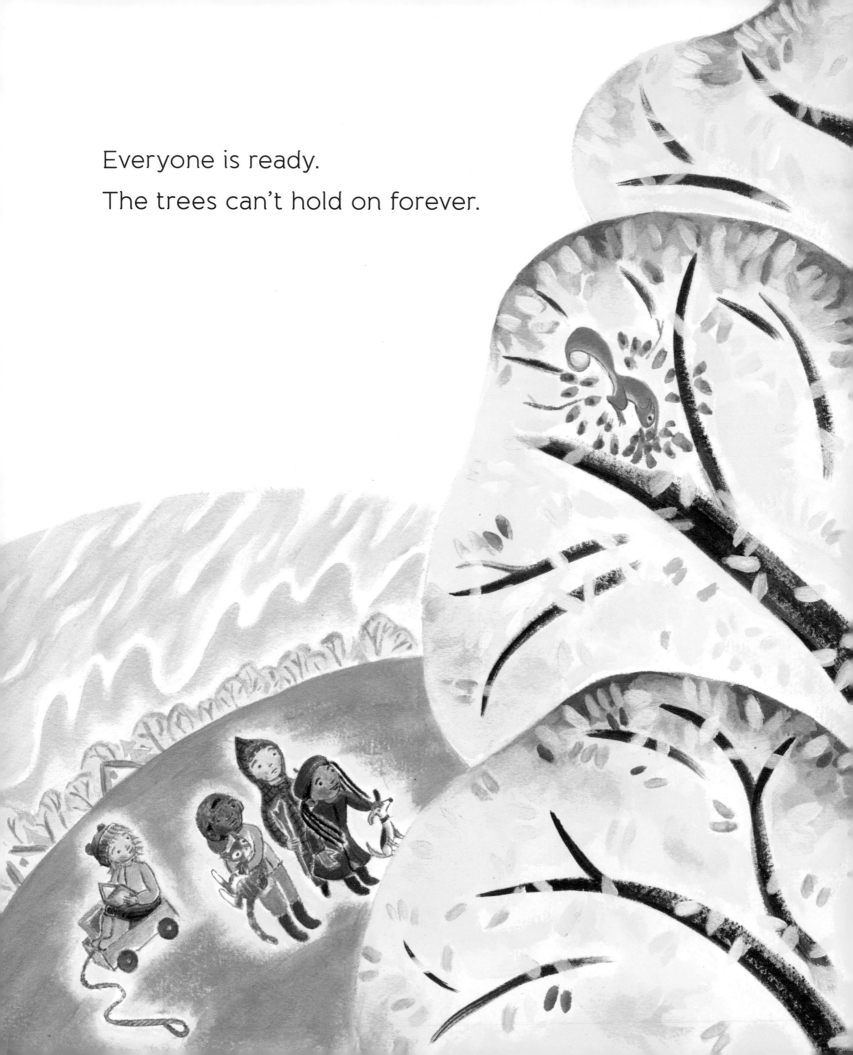

The sky billows gray with clouds,
and then it begins. . . .

The wind blows
yellow sideways,
then up,
then down.

Everywhere fills
with yellow.
A symphony
of yellow.

Children run in
the yellow air.
They let it catch their hair
and cover their sweaters.
They jump and turn
in yellow time.

It only comes
once a year.

And when it is over,
piles of yellow
pool in gutters,
decorate sidewalks,
blanket fences, steps, roofs,
even an empty birdbath.

Black crows fill bare branches
and raise their voices
in praise of yellow time.

Squirrels, still busy, bundle final touches of yellow to their high, leafy nests, while children below gather bouquets of yellow . . .

to press in thick books

to remember . . .

what a lovely yellow time it was.

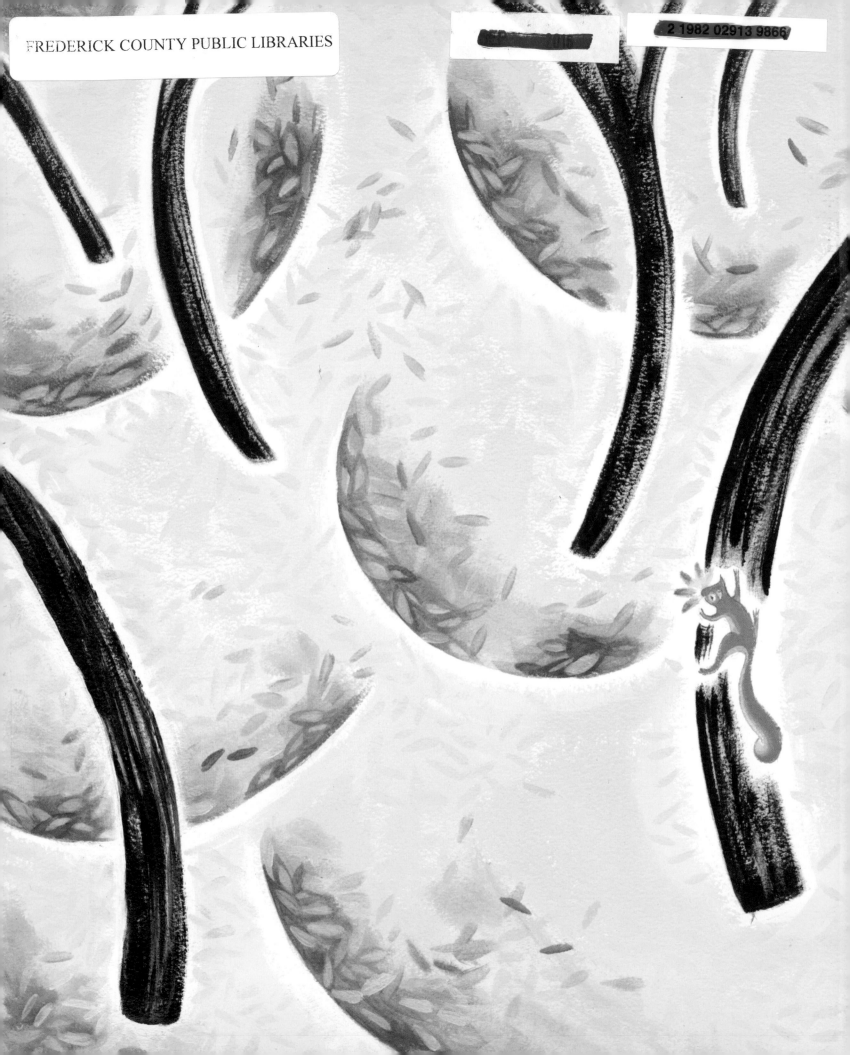